The Pegasus Club and Me

Story by Amanda Beck

Illustrations by Yoshi Miyake

RAINTREE
STECK-VAUGHN
LIBRARY

Austin, Texas

I dedicate this book with love to my family:
Byron, Dorothy, and Adam Beck.—**A.B.**

To Rosamond Edison.—**Y.M.**

Library of Congress Cataloging-in-Publication Data

Beck, Amanda, 1979-
  The Pegasus Club and me / story by Amanda Beck;
illustrations by Yoshi Miyake.
    p. cm. —(Publish a book)
  Summary: Amy must choose between becoming
friends with a classmate or remaining in the exclusive
Pegasus Club.
    1. Children's writings. (1. Clubs—Fiction. 2. Friendship—
Fiction. 3. Schools—Fiction. 4. Children's writings.)
I. Miyake, Yoshi, ill. II. Title. III. Series.
PZ7.B380766Pe   1992   (Fic)—dc20   91-38330
                                                                      CIP
ISBN 0-8114-3577-6   AC

I'm Amy Wallace and I don't care one red cent about that ol' Pegasus Club anymore. Period.

I go to the Modia Millicks school and everybody has club fever again, same as last year—the same year that I joined the Pegasus Club and left it. You want to know why? I'll tell you.

Last year, when the club-fever bug was biting, the Pegasus Club got started by some low-down, shifty-eyed girls who I thought at that time were "pretty." They collected dues, giggled about boys, clothes, and hair styles, and argued over which singing group is the hottest—stuff like that.

A few days after this group got started, they sent out a notice to every classroom.

So the next day, along with about ten other girls, I was at the gym by 3:15, in my nicest school clothes and carrying my flute. By 3:30 I had played the "Serenade" by F. J. Haydn without missing a note.

When we were all done, Devin Delaney, the Pegasus vice president, said, "Meet here at the gym tomorrow and we'll tell you if you made the club." Then she linked arms with the other officers and they chattered themselves out the door, leaving us all in suspense.

The next day Chrissy Boenlay herself, the
Pegasus president, came up to me and said,
"Well, Amy, you're really lucky—you made
the club."

For initiation I had to wear my sweatshirt
inside out and get some boy's phone number
for Devin, but for the first month the club was
tolerably nice to me, and lots of fun.

15

Then Sarah Larken came, an ordinary girl in all ways but one. She could sing like a lark.

I guess it was because of her voice that the Pegasus officers wanted Sarah to join the club. She was invited to the next meeting, where she found out that she'd have to do an initiation stunt.

"All you have to do," Chrissy said, "is steal Mrs. Lenden's grade book and bring it back to us."

Everyone gasped. None of us had TOUCHED the sacred grade book. We didn't dare.

"**W**hat?!?" gasped Sarah, her eyes filling up with tears. "What?"

"You heard me," said Chrissy, "and if you really want to be in the club, you will."

"No," Sarah cried, "I don't want to be in the club after all." Then, bursting into tears, she ran out of the gym.

I felt kind of sad for her, but Devin and Chrissy were mad! They had never dreamed someone would decide NOT to join the club. They were still mouthing off when I left for my flute lesson.

Two days later our teacher, Mrs. Lenden, stormed into the classroom.

"All right!" she said, making us jump. "I put my grade book in my desk last night, and now my drawers are a mess and the grade book's gone. Who took it?"

No one answered, so she carefully searched all our desks, grunting each time she did not find it.

But when she finally stuck her hand into Sarah's desk, she gave a yell of triumph and held the small black book high in the air. Then she looked at a pale, appalled, astounded, and trembling Sarah and said the words no child wants to hear.

"You, miss, are in very big trouble."

I opened my mouth to protest. I had been with Sarah when school got out, and we had walked home together. But before I could say anything, Devin Delaney gave me a look—a look that said plainer than words, "Keep your mouth shut or you and the Pegasus Club are HISTORY."

I hesitated. Being in the Pegasus Club meant that I was one of the special few. I had status, importance. To lose the Pegasus Club meant that I would be an ordinary girl again.

An ordinary girl with a special friend…

I looked at Sarah. So small beside the looming shape of Mrs. Lenden, she seemed to be pleading with me. How could I leave her to the terrible fate that awaited her?

I couldn't!

And I didn't.

Now I spoke out loud and clear. "Mrs. Lenden, Sarah couldn't have done it. I was with her yesterday afternoon, and Davy Boardmann from the fourth grade was with us."

It didn't take long to convince her that Sarah was innocent. But she couldn't figure out who really did it, and I didn't tell her. I figured the real culprits would get their comeuppance, without any help from me, sooner or later.

Well, the Pegasus Club has lasted to this day just fine without me, and I don't envy the girls in it. Now I have my own bunch of real friends, but my best friend is still Sarah Larken.

Amanda Beck was born in London, England, in October 1979, when her parents were students there at University College. They returned to Rock Island, Illinois, when she was a baby, and she has lived there ever since. Rock Island is part of Quad-Cities, USA, where the Sauk and Fox Indians lived, died, and buried their dead, and where the Mississippi River flows from east to west. There are museums, orchestras, libraries, colleges, and shopping malls, just like big cities, but farmland is only five minutes' drive away.

Amanda finds plenty to do in Rock Island. She can ski and toboggan in the winter (on big hills, not mountains), and ride horses, swim, and canoe in the summer. She lives with her brother, Adam, who is eight, and her parents, Byron and Dorothy. She has a beautiful but dumb dog, Misty, and an eccentric rabbit. Amanda is part of a group that does English rapier sword dancing and performs for church groups and madrigals. She plays the piano at home and the flute in the school band. She loves music—playing it, singing it, or listening to it. She has been in Girl Scouts since she was seven. She has learned a lot as a Scout and likes the opportunities it gives her to be useful in the community. She also likes collecting miniatures for her doll house and just playing with her brother. But more than anything else, Amanda loves reading. She likes writing, too; she wrote her first story when she was in kindergarten. But ever since she was about four, her absolutely favorite thing to do has been to read.

Amanda first heard about the Publish-a-Book contest from Juanita Wahe at the Rock Island library. The librarian knew that Amanda liked to read and encouraged her to enter. Amanda started writing **The Pegasus Club and Me** that same day. She thought perhaps she'd get an honorable mention, but she never dreamed her story would be published.

Amanda has thought about what she'd like to be when she's older, but she keeps changing her mind. Sometimes she thinks she'd like to be a pharmacist. Or maybe she'll be a librarian. Or maybe a park ranger...

The twenty honorable-mention winners in the **1991 Raintree/Steck-Vaughn Publish-a-Book Contest** were Wendy Leigh Bleyl of Houston, Texas; Sybrina Brantley of Crossett, Arkansas; Katie Drury of Troy, Michigan; Brittany Erkman of Annapolis, Maryland; Laura Jagusch of Dearborn Heights, Michigan; Nathan Knell of Duncanville, Texas; Jeremy Mistretta of Houston, Texas; Matthew Moffa of Ligonier, Pennsylvania; Amy Nawatka of South Milwaukee, Wisconsin; Pamela Parris of New Hampshire; Katie Reinart of Cincinnati, Ohio; Lori Scrudato of Bayonne, New Jersey; Cam Sele of Fairbanks, Alaska; Jennifer Shaffer of Weatherford, Oklahoma; Nicole Shiraishi of Kailua, Hawaii; Tori Smith of Walkerton, Indiana; W. Destin Veach-Cook of Duncanville, Texas; Jaclyn Webb of Moore, Oklahoma; Laurie Winston of Milford, Connecticut; and Amanda Lee Yeager of Belle, West Virginia.

Artist Yoshi Miyake was born in Tokyo into a family of artists. In 1966, she came to the United States to study design and illustration. The major body of her work consists of children's books. Yoshi loves to travel in the western states, and she collects American Indian art. She lives in Chicago with her Doberman pinscher, Bucky.